KU-796-359

HEDGEHOGS

MINNA TAYLOR

Auntie Lizzie's Lion

illustrated by
Glenys Ambrus

HODDER AND STOUGHTON
London   Sydney   Auckland   Toronto

British Library Cataloguing in Publication Data

Taylor, Minna
    Auntie Lizzie's lion.
    I. Title   II. Ambrus, Glenys   III. Series
    823'.914 [J]

    ISBN 0-340-51401-9

First published 1990

Published by Hodder and Stoughton Children's Books,
a division of Hodder and Stoughton Ltd,
Mill Road, Dunton Green, Sevenoaks, Kent TN13 2YA

Photoset by En to En, Tunbridge Wells, Kent

Printed in Great Britain by Cambus Litho, East Kilbride

It was Wednesday and James hurried along
to Auntie Lizzie's house after school.
He wondered if Barnabas would be there.
Barnabas was Auntie Lizzie's pet lion.
He was terribly spoiled.
   Auntie Lizzie had taken Barnabas to stay
with her when the circus closed down.
She called him Barney for short.

You need a special kind of licence to keep a lion. Auntie Lizzie had put hers in a frame and hung it above the mantelpiece.

Auntie Lizzie had left the door unlocked for James. He turned the handle and walked in. 'It's me. It's me, Auntie Lizzie,' he shouted and ran into the living-room.

'What a noise you make, James MacGregor,' she said. 'Can't you see Barney's not well?'

Barnabas was lying on the settee with
Auntie Lizzie's best travelling rug on top of
him, the one she brought back from Oban
last year. She was giving him a spoonful of
gruel. It was a sort of grey-looking mixture,
like very thin porridge. James thought it
looked revolting.

Barnabas turned his head away. James
didn't blame him.

'What's wrong with him, Auntie Lizzie?'
James asked. 'Can I have my lemonade
and biscuits now?' There was a glass of
lemonade and two digestive biscuits on the
table.

Barnabas groaned.
'Have you no sense, James MacGregor?'
Auntie Lizzie said. 'Mentioning lemonade
and biscuits when Barney's right off his
food. It's enough to make him sick.'
Barnabas groaned again.

James drank his lemonade down in one gulp. He turned the biscuits over to see if there was chocolate on the other side. There wasn't. He ate one.

When he reached for the second one it wasn't there. It had vanished. He looked everywhere but there was no sign of it.

Barnabas was licking some crumbs off his face. I bet Barnabas is just pretending to be sick, James thought. He wondered why.

James remembered he had pretended to be sick once when he didn't want to go to school. But he was so hungry by lunch-time that he had to recover very quickly in order to get something to eat.

Auntie Lizzie took a large grey raincoat from the cupboard. It was an old one of Grandpa Briggs's.

'Perhaps a breath of fresh air will do him good,' she said. 'You can make yourself useful and take him for a walk.'

James sighed.

Barnabas pricked up his ears when he heard the word 'walk' and James saw him smile.

Auntie Lizzie put Barnabas's two front
paws through the sleeves of the raincoat
and fastened the buttons underneath him.
The collar stuck out round his neck like a
frill. 'I don't want Barney to catch cold,'
she said.

Barnabas looked at himself in the mirror and fluttered his eyes. James thought he looked ridiculous. Whoever saw a lion in a raincoat?

Then Auntie Lizzie put on his lead and handed James a ladies' umbrella with a long handle. 'Put that over Barney's head if it rains,' she said. 'Now off you go. Just round the block and no further. And DON'T give him anything to eat.'

As soon as Auntie Lizzie shut the door, Barnabas raced for the stairs, pulling James behind him. He didn't look at all ill.

People laughed when they saw a lion in a raincoat and James felt very embarrassed. He tried to hide Auntie Lizzie's umbrella behind his back, but he couldn't hide Barnabas.

When they reached the corner shop
Barnabas sat down in front of the door and
refused to move. Nobody could get in or
out. Soon a queue began to form.

18

James tugged at the lead but Barnabas would not budge. Angry voices shouted 'Move along there' and 'I've got a train to catch'. James didn't know what to do.

19

Mrs MacAllister, the owner of the shop, came out to see what all the commotion was about. 'Why, it's Barney waiting for his bar of chocolate,' she said. 'He always gets one when Auntie Lizzie comes in to pay for her papers.'

She popped a bar of chocolate into Barnabas's mouth. He sucked it slowly, licking his lips afterwards. Then he clapped his two front paws together. Mrs MacAllister didn't offer any to James.

When the rain came on James put the umbrella up over Barnabas's head. It was bright red with blue flowers. He knew Auntie Lizzie would be cross if Barnabas got wet.

He got all the drips down his neck. They ran down his nose and left a big long drip at the end of it.

The ice-cream van was sitting at the side of the road, but no one wanted ice-cream. It was too wet.

Barnabas snatched the umbrella from James and balanced it on the end of his nose. Then he stood on his hind legs and twirled it round and round. The drips went everywhere and splashed a smartly-dressed lady who was walking past. She wasn't very pleased.

People gathered round to watch,
and started to buy ice-cream.

The ice-cream man was delighted.
He handed James a giant cone. 'Here, give
that to your lion, sonny,' he said. 'I haven't
done such good business on a wet day for
a long time.'

Barnabas gobbled down the ice-cream.
He didn't even offer James a lick.
He seemed to have completely recovered.
If there was ever anything wrong with him,
thought James. 'Serve you right if you're
really sick,' he said to Barnabas.

The ice-cream man tapped James on the
shoulder. 'Have a cone yourself, son. On the
house,' he said with a wink.

When they came to Auntie Lizzie's door,
Barnabas pretended to be sick again.
He walked slowly into the room and lay
down in front of the fire. He gave a loud
groan.

'Poor Barney,' said Auntie Lizzie. 'You still
look a bit peelie-wally. You certainly won't be
able to go off to that safari park
tomorrow.'

Barnabas groaned again and James understood why he was pretending to be sick. He wanted to stay where he was.

'He'll just have to stay with you, Auntie Lizzie,' James said.

Barnabas smiled.